Presented to

_____

from

_____

_____

*19*___

The King's Manners

A Bible Book about Courtesy

The King's Manners

Library of Congress Cataloging-in-Publication Data

Hollingsworth, Mary, 1947-
The king's manners : a Bible book about courtesy / concept by
Cheryl Rico and Ginger Knight ; illustrated by Mary Grace
Eubank ; text by Mary Hollingsworth.
p. cm.
Summary: A rhyming introduction to courtesy and manners
through God's declaration of the Golden Rule.
ISBN 0-8499-0826-4
[1. Etiquette — Fiction. 2. Conduct of life — Fiction.
3. Christian life — Fiction.] I. Rico, Cheryl, 1951- . II. Knight,
Ginger, 1954- . III. Eubank, Mary Grace, ill. IV. Title.
PZ8.3.H7196Kj   1990

[E] — dc20   90-32210
                                                              CIP
                                                               AC

Printed in the United States of America

1239LB9876543

The King's Manners

A Bible Book about Courtesy

Concept by: Cheryl Rico and Ginger Knight
Illustrated by: Mary Grace Eubank
Text by: Mary Hollingsworth

WORD PUBLISHING
Dallas · London · Vancouver · Melbourne

Dear Parent,

As a concerned parent, you know that good manners are some of the most desirable behaviors we can teach our children. Even the youngest child needs to learn how to share, to be polite and to treat others kindly. Manners lay the groundwork for good communication that will last a lifetime.

The King's Manners teaches basic courtesy such as saying "please" and "thank you," plus it shows children to pray before they eat, be quiet in church and use their manners to serve God. The delightful illustrations by world-famous Sesame Street artist, Mary Grace Eubank, captivate children's attention. The clever rhyming text by Mary Hollingsworth is fun to hear or read aloud.

We hope **The King's Manners** will be an invaluable tool to teach good manners to the children you love. It will be a fun experience for you both!

The Publisher

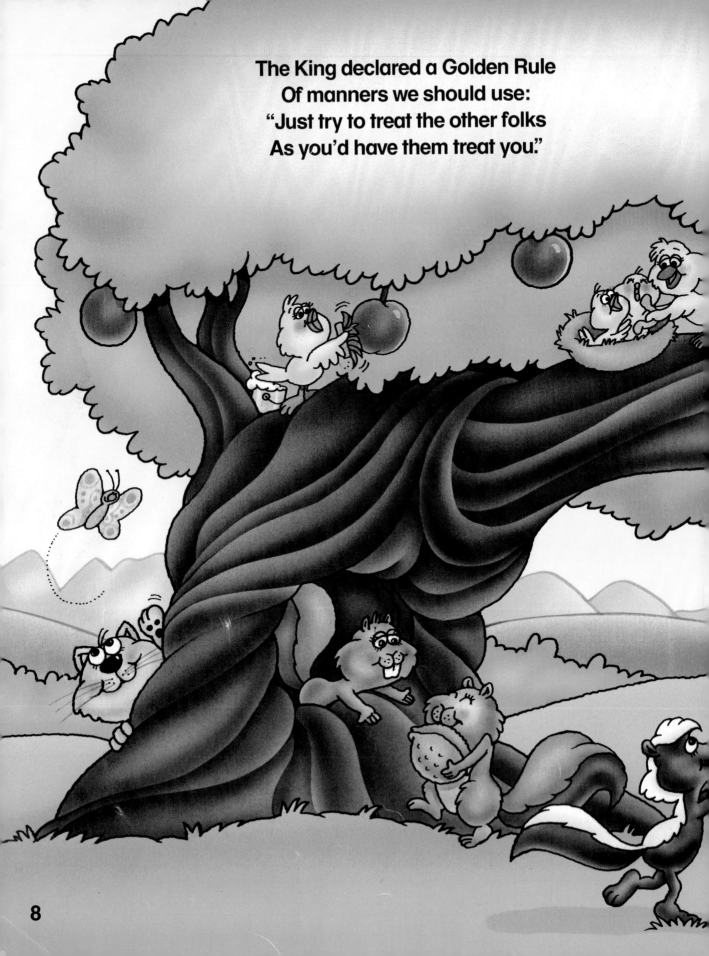

The King declared a Golden Rule
Of manners we should use:
"Just try to treat the other folks
As you'd have them treat you."

So say a "please," or say a "thanks"
At home or church or school.
Good manners will come back to you.
'Cause that's the Golden Rule!

Trees.
Breeze.
Buzzing bees.
Honey's nice, like saying "please."
Bee-ware,
Mr. Bear!
Say, "May I, pretty please?"

Now, honey's sweet 'n sappy,
But bees will turn you slappy,
And breezes make the leaves go flappy.
And last of all, but best of all,
Your "please" makes God so happy.

Yoohoo!
Yes, you!
Say, "Thank you, that was nice."
When you receive a gift,
Say, "Thank you" once or twice.

Yoohoo!
Yes, you!
Good manners are a treat.
When someone's kind, just take the time—
Say, "Thank you, that was sweet."

13

Our God is great.
Our God is good.

I know I should.
I'm sure I should

Say "Thank you, God"
Before I sleep.

And "Thank you, God"
Before I eat.

14

I'm sure I should.
I know I should,

For God is great,
And God is good.

There's times you sneeze
Or cough or wheeze.
(Are you allergic to Siamese?)
Well, when you sneeze
Or cough or wheeze
Then say, "Excuse me, please."

If you should hear your friend's "Ahhhh chew!"
Whatever should you do?
A laugh won't do;
No big to-do;
Just say, "God bless you, Sue."

Fumble, bumble,
You might stumble
Into someone in your way.

Do not grumble.
Do not mumble.
"Sorry, friend," is what you say.

On one trapeze
Flew three Chinese
With the very greatest ease.
On trapeze two
Chimpanzees flew
From Timbuktu's big zoo.

20

When one trapeze,
That caught the breeze,
Bumped into trapeze two,
"Chimpanzees," said the three Chinese,
"Excuse our bumping you!"

It's great to share as Jesus shared,
And things to share are everywhere—
Our toys and food and buzzing bugs,
And lots of fuzzy-wuzzy hugs.

22

When you have two,
But she has none,
Then give her one to use.
Now, this works well —
In fact, it's swell —
Unless it's sleeves or shoes!

23

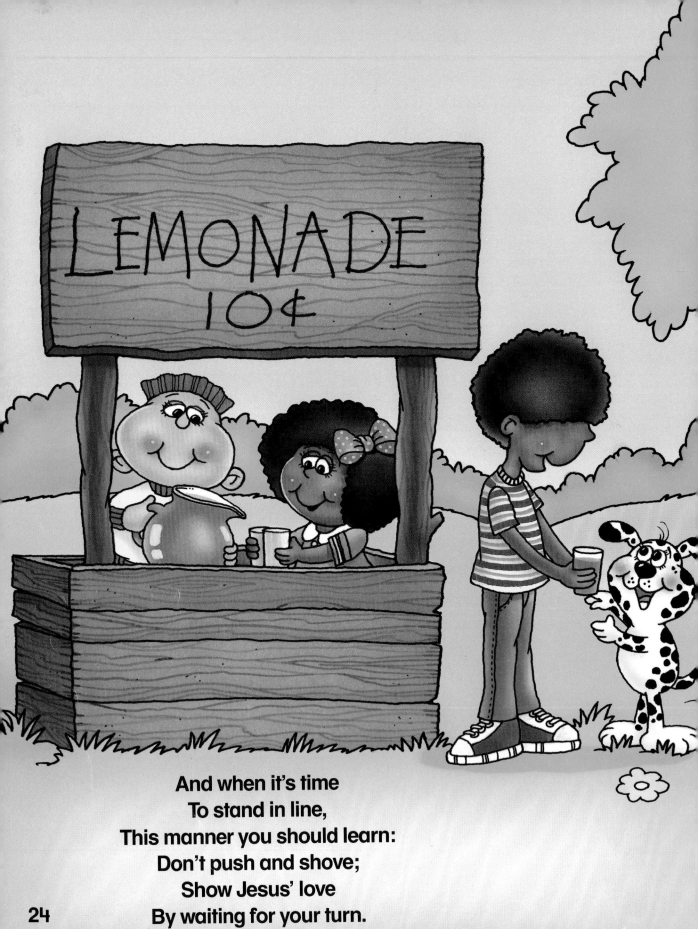

And when it's time
To stand in line,
This manner you should learn:
Don't push and shove;
Show Jesus' love
By waiting for your turn.

Or when you have an awful thirst,
And Terry's thirsty, too,
Let him go first to quench his thirst,
And he'll think good of you.

Tiptoe, tiptoe softly, please,
Each time you're in God's house.
And when you hear the Bible read,
Be quiet as a mouse.

Now, when you hear somebody pray,
It's not the time to play.
Just listen very quietly
To hear what he will say.

27

You've played and had a happy day;
So, put your toys away.
Please put them in the storage box —
Your favorite doll with golden locks,
Your funny clown with stripety socks,
Your trains and trucks and building blocks.
See, helping is good manners, too,
And Jesus will be proud of you!

It's time for bed,
You sleepyhead.
Today is almost gone.
Don't cry and fuss;
You can't fool us—
We saw that great big yawn.

30

Take Teddy, Scruffy and Old Joe,
And get your baseball glove.
Your sweet "good night" is so polite,
God smiles from up above.

31

Good manners are so nice to use;
They cause God's world to sing!
So make your life go better
With the manners of the King.